For Megan
She's a new baby who's just arrived!

Published by
PEACHTREE PUBLISHERS, LTD.
1700 Chattahoochee Avenue
Atlanta, Georgia 30318-2112

www.peachtree-online.com

Text and illustrations © 2002 John Butler

Illustrations created in acrylic and colored pencil

First published in Great Britain in 2002 by Orchard Books

Manufactured in Singapore

10 9 8 7 6 5 4 3 2 1
First Edition

ISBN 1-56145-269-6

Cataloging-in-Publication Data is available from the Library of Congress

Hush, Little Ones

John Butler

PEACHTREE

ATLANTA

Hush, little ones,
you sleepyheads,
Warm and safe
in your own special beds.

Hush, little rabbits, don't make a sound.

Sleep tight in your burrow, deep underground.

Hush, little monkey,
rest your head,
As Mother climbs up
to your treetop bed.

Hush, little mice, it's time to rest,

Snug in the hollow of your cozy nest.

Hush, little lions, no time for play.
Cuddle up close at the end of the day.

Hush, little penguin, go to sleep,
Nestled between your father's feet.

Hush, little kangaroo, close your eyes.

Drift into dreams as the moon starts to rise.

Hush, little bear cubs, bedtime is here,

Warm in your den where Mother is near.

Hush, little zebra, you'll be dozing soon,

By the light of the stars and the silvery moon.

Hush, little ducklings, curl up tight.

Snuggle together all through the night.

Hush, little whale, in the deep, blue sea.

It's lullaby time for you and me.

Hush, little ones,
in the pale moonlight.
It's dream time now,
good night, sleep tight.